PECULIAR PETS

Poetry Treasures

Edited By Bobby Tobolik

First published in Great Britain in 2021 by:

Young Writers
Remus House
Coltsfoot Drive
Peterborough
PE2 9BF
Telephone: 01733 890066
Website: www.youngwriters.co.uk

Printed and bound in the UK by BookPrintingUK
Website: www.bookprintinguk.com
YB0455J

FOREWORD

Welcome Reader!

Are you ready to discover weird and wonderful
creatures that you'd never even dreamed of?

For Young Writers' latest competition we asked primary
school pupils to create a Peculiar Pet of their own
invention, and then write a poem about it! They rose to
the challenge magnificently and the result is this fantastic
collection full of creepy critters and amazing animals!

Here at Young Writers our aim is to encourage creativity
in children and to inspire a love of the written word, so
it's great to get such an amazing response, with some
absolutely fantastic poems. Not only have these young
authors created imaginative and inventive animals, they've
also crafted wonderful poems to showcase their creations
and their writing ability. These poems are brimming with
inspiration. The slimiest slitherers, the creepiest crawlers
and furriest friends are all brought to life in these pages –
you can decide for yourself which ones you'd like as a pet!

I'd like to congratulate all the young authors
in this anthology, I hope this inspires them
to continue with their creative writing.

★ CONTENTS ★

Limpsfield Junior School, Sheffield

Majid Amponsem (10)	55
Amarn Zamil (8)	56
Sophie Rae Mitchell (10)	57
Nirvana Phipps (10)	58
Diamond Haughton (9)	59
Feyzi Sozen (10)	60
Kai Huxtable (10)	61
Briah Buch (8)	62
Gabriel Quist (10)	63
Amelia Basharat	64
Stanley Joe Priest (10)	65
Savannah Johnson (9)	66
Aimee Bridges (8)	67
Ayaan Ali Ashraf (10)	68
Lucca Schofield (8)	69
Rumaysa Saqib (10)	70
Henna Mortada (11)	71
William Fernando (10)	72
Haashir Saqib (9)	73
Taylor Parnell (8)	74
Ethan Baxter (8)	75
Ogechi Ejiogu (9)	76
Darciee Malcolm O'Sullivan (11)	77
Abigail Grace Nicholls (10)	78
Soraya Abdou (8)	79
Beth Aston (8)	80
Amina Mamboleo (9)	81
Roman Mitchell (7)	82
Alfie Gibson (10)	83
Emily Nicholls (7)	84
Aishah Rashid (7)	85
Ollie Staniforth	86
Charis Weston (8)	87
Bilal Abrouche (9)	88
Elisia Nkereko (9)	89
Minsa Farhan (8)	90
Lilly Smith (7)	91
Ruby Lockwood (9)	92
Zak Zahid (8)	93
Hannah Chitopo (8)	94
Lillie Greaves (8)	95

Alayah Khan (10)	96
Scarlett Crowther (8)	97
Jacob Dunning (10)	98
Ahmed Syed (9)	99
Jacob Duffy (8)	100
Shafiyah Amina Bashir (8)	101
Israa Miah (10)	102
Faye Bennett (10)	103
Florence Joel-Drennan (9)	104
Riley Marsland (8)	105
Aahil Khan (8)	106
Muskaan Hussain (11)	107
Joshua Smith (8)	108
Heidi Rodgers (8)	109
Esmond Thompson (9)	110
Akira Wilkinson (8)	111
Zak Fox (10)	112
Madison Brough (8)	113
Darcie Wake (9)	114
Ikhlas Mah (8)	115

Oakington Manor Primary School, Wembley

Tabasem Azizi (8)	116
Promise Soda (8)	118
Maximilian Paulo Lule (9)	119
Fathima Begum (8)	120
Azaan Asim (8)	121
Quiana Quaye-Murray (8)	122
Ubaidullah Butt (9)	123
Musa Nadim (9)	124
Courtney Rebecca Jackson (9)	125
Jameelah Abyan (8)	126
Yasin Mumtaz Ahmed (8)	127
Ojashwee Maharjan (9)	128
Saleeha Mirza (8)	129
Arham Ahmed Awan (8)	130

The Harbour School, Wilburton

Lennon Snitch (10)	131
Jesse Nunley Towers (11)	132
Caleb Harrington (9)	133

THE POEMS

Whiskers The Perfect Pet!

W hiskers is a perfect pet

H alf ocelot, half chihuahua, she always loves to play

I n the day she likes to run and have lots of fun!

S he is forever ready for a treat, her favourite happens to be chicken meat

K nowingly she glares at me with her yellow and blue eyes

E very night she purrs and barks to sleep

R unning with her best friends

S ocks the silly sheep and Baba the super fat sheep!

Lucy Jessica MacGregor (11)
Abernyte Primary School, Inchture

Aguanacorn

A dorable, it is helpful and kind
G entle and slimy, quiet and cute
U nder the umbrella doing the cha-cha
A mazing, it shines, it is invisible too
N ever cheeky, lazy and colourful
A lways playing on Fortnite getting victory royales
C orn on a cob it eats all day long
O n a sheep sleeping
R iding all day long
N ight-vision goggles it uses.

Rory Strickland (8)
Abernyte Primary School, Inchture

Merlumos

M agical like her eyes in the sun
E nergetic to play and run around
R unning in the wind she plays happily
L oving and fluffy like a pillow
U nique like me
M y dream pet is her
O utstanding like a trophy
S uper swimmer like a professional.

Emma Bailey (10)
Abernyte Primary School, Inchture

Rocky The Rainbow Rhino

R ocky the rainbow rhino always likes to play
O utstanding in every way, as bright as the sun
C olourful like a rainbow every single day
K ind and thoughtful, lovely all the time
Y ucky is not a word for him as he walks tiredly.

Euan Strickland (10)
Abernyte Primary School, Inchture

Pig-Duck

Its pink head bobbing up and down
You'd expect by now it would've drowned.
It swims to the coast and climbs ashore,
To reveal that it is no ordinary pig or boar.

It scrambles onto ground with its dark webbed feet
And waddles on to its own beat.
A duck or a pig? Perhaps it's both
Maybe the two animals made some kind of oath.

A flock of swans fled at the sight
Of the pig that was paddling with all its might.
They all hid in a patch of grass
While the pig attempted to eat a fish,
That seemed to be a black bass.

The feet of a bird and the head of a pig
It walked up the shore and tripped over a twig.
It stumbled back onto its wobbling toes,
Waddling into some greenery and off it goes.

Sophia K (11)
Chantry Middle School, Morpeth

A Potato Rat

This rat is yellow and round and it could talk,
Its brother looks like pork,
What's this vision, is it true? I started to wake,
I woke up from my weird dream, my dad came to
say,
That my friend had said, "Come and play."
When I came back, there was a moving potato,
My dad said, "Where's the tomato?"
I picked the potato up really quickly, it squirmed
like a snake,
My dad said, "Where's the potato? I need it to
bake."
I put the potato in a cage,
I dropped my book in the cage, the rat turned the
page,
I finally saw its face, it was cute until I saw its
mouth,
It was big and green and gooey,
My dad said, "The floor is rather sticky."
I said back, "I don't know why."
My dad said, "Where's that potato? I need to make
a pie."

My friend came by the next day,
I said, "You can't come into my room because you
have to pay."
My friend said, "Why, why, why? Oh why?"

Joshua H (11)
Chantry Middle School, Morpeth

Scaredy-Cat

Smidge is my pet cat,
And he loves his mat.
But there is something about him,
Which will make you not want him.

Deep in the night,
You will get a fright.
From pans falling on the floor,
And scratching at your door.

He is allergic to everything,
And flea treatment that really does smell ming.
Every morning when we open the door,
There's always sick on the floor.

The neighbours keep on shooing him away,
And unfortunately, we have to pay.
We have to pay to fix the gate,
And all the food he had ate.

He always goes to number nine,
And all that we hear is, "Hey, that's mine!"
So if you see him being disgusting,
You better start running.

Madeleine Brewis (11)
Chantry Middle School, Morpeth

Seal Sausage

The seal sausage,
It rolls along the great, long road
A magnificent sight
For all who see it while in the night.
Its body is smooth like a cheap balloon,
Its legs are non-existent
Like they are hiding from a virus
Super Noodle whiskers shoot out of its cheeks,
Eyes are like a surprise on the seal sausage
Changing like a disco ball every five seconds
Its favourite show ranges far and wide
But overall, isn't much of a surprise.
His best friend is Fishy Fly
Everyone loves the seal sausage.

Megan P (11)
Chantry Middle School, Morpeth

Mindy The Ugly Rat

Mindy the jumping naked rat.

Springs around her space,
Looking for someone maybe human race.

Someone who she can love,
Someone as pretty as a dove.

But no one wants to go near,
Her teeth are big and she's always been feared.

Her pink naked skin,
Does not determine what's within!

Judging a book by its cover,
Isn't someone who is fit to be a lover.

Seek for good on the inside,
And maybe you'll get a big surprise.

Elle D (11)
Chantry Middle School, Morpeth

Merkitty!

M atching tail to her body
E very day she is down at the ocean
R acing her friends, she beats all of them
K eeping watch of the fish
I sland exploring is her favourite
T ouch her tail and she will scratch you
T ell her you love her, she will be happy
Y ou will love Merkitty and her tail of course.

Grace H (11)

Chantry Middle School, Morpeth

Snarantula

A slimy, slithery snake,
Mixed with a terrifying tarantula.
Yes, imagine that!
Its creepy, crawly legs
And the slithering, slimy snake
Crawling all the way up your back.

It is two foot long,
And is so very strong.
It is horrific but cool,
I would have this snarantula
And I bet you would too!

Marlie S (11)
Chantry Middle School, Morpeth

Grimpotius

G ood little swimmers
R arely in trouble
I mpressively cute
M ore like an octopus
P lenty of tentacles
O ctopuses are its sibling
T he thing isn't big
I mmersed in the depths
U nited with its family
S uper cute.

Will S (11)
Chantry Middle School, Morpeth

The Sloth Flash

F ast and furious
L ovable rogue
A lways in a rush against time
S peed is key
H e's a unit.

Ewan T (11)
Chantry Middle School, Morpeth

My Pet Peter

I have a funny little bird called Peter,
Who is a feathery, lazy tweeter,
He just refuses to fly,
I really don't know how he will get by,
He sits in his cage on his perch,
So at least we don't have to search,
He's a marvellous, cute but messy bird,
I find him quite absurd,
I hope one day he will flap his wings,
So he will see what joy it brings,
He's a weird, peculiar pet,
But he's the best I can get,
He tries to fly and flaps his wings,
But all he does is fly into things.

Jess Fowler (8)
Cromer Junior School, Cromer

Sun Wolf

S ometimes I go for a moonlit stroll
U nfortunately, I saw no animals
N ext day, I went for a sunshine stroll on the way
to school

W hen I saw it, I was aghast. Not a unicorn or a
dinosaur...
O n a giant rock in the park, I saw a wolf, it was
doing
L ots of howling, not at the moon, the sun!
F our children had also seen this amazing sight of
the sun wolf, an amazing creature!

Willow Davis (8)
Cromer Junior School, Cromer

Power Primrose

I'm Power Primrose, I am so spotty,
I like being dotty.
Super pets eat chocolate bars,
Me and my friends catch falling stars.
Oh, it's good not to be scared at night,
When it's time, I take flight!
Even super dogs need a nice, warm bath,
With my red cape, I saved a cute baby calf.

Rose Katerina Modle (8)
Cromer Junior School, Cromer

Mischievous Milly The Cat

Mischievous Milly steals cheese from mice,
Hisses and growls at anyone she sees,
Although she thinks she is a horse,
Jumps hurdles and she eats hay,
She eats carrots, bites people
And thinks she has a long snout,
She has sharp scales, furry skin,
Feathery hooves and tiny ears.

Mollie Taylor (9)
Cromer Junior School, Cromer

Long-Eared Dog

L oving
O dd
N apping
G olden retriever

E nergetic
A thletic
R acing rabbits
E very
D ay

D elightful
O ld
G irl!

Jessica Harding (8)
Cromer Junior School, Cromer

The Magical Day

M arvellous pegasus called Magic

A rrived at a boy called Pattric

G oing to meet a lovely princess, Pattric put on his best clothes

I n the castle full of sparkle

C rystals brightened their magical day.

Olga Fox (8)

Cromer Junior School, Cromer

The Big Fat Ginger Cat

My cat is ginger
He thinks he's a ninja
His special power is that he can fly
He swooshes on by
He's the fastest cat
But unfortunately, he's fat
He's cuddly and sweet
But most of all, he likes meat.

Poppy Spanton (8)
Cromer Junior School, Cromer

Super Primrose

I'm Super Dog,
I can walk on a log,
I can save people and animals out of fog.
I have dots,
People call them spots.
I have a love heart nose,
I can do a Super Primrose pose.

Ruby Sophia Modle (8)
Cromer Junior School, Cromer

Super Snake

S uper Snake is here
N apping in the day
A t night, he puts on his cape
K een to help you out
E ating rats and mice until the morning light.

Jacob Grant (8)
Cromer Junior School, Cromer

The Fearless Chicken

There's a fearless chicken in this town,
His name is Dave and he's a clown,
When I mean a clown, I mean a clown,
He jumps off cliffs and he doesn't hear a sound.

Andre Bandarra (8)
Cromer Junior School, Cromer

My Croc

C roc has shiny scales and is very fond of beluga whales

R ock stars call him a croc star, but he isn't that bizarre

O ceans are presents to him because he really likes to swim

C heeky crocs love rocks, but my Croc weirdly wears frocks!

M y Croc does not snap and I would certainly not give him a slap

Y aks however really want him to snap, but he won't, not even if you give him a smack

P eople disliked Croc because he gave them a shock

E lephants are dangerous to Croc because they kept giving him a knock

T he loop the loop he tries to do, but he never gets to zigzag through the blue.

Lucy Aurora Torres-Catmur (8)
Drapers' Maylands Primary School, Harold Hill

My Flying Elephant

My flying elephant friend, won't you stay?
I'll help and play with you every day.
Where are you going to go?
Outside it's very heavy snow.
Oh please, my dear friend, don't go, I'm home alone,
Just stay until my parents get home.
Look, I just found my blue comb.
That just reminded me, where is my cloak?
Wait, I left it outside, oh it must be soaked.
It's cold outside you know,
So you better stay or you might blow away.
Stay until it stops snowing, so we can play for most of the day.

Jazmine Clare (8)
Drapers' Maylands Primary School, Harold Hill

Candyfloss

C olourful unicorns are colourful only in the night

A s I was walking to school I saw loads of unicorns

N earby I always see loads of unicorns, they live near to me

D o you ever see a unicorn?

Y ellow unicorns are the peach coloured unicorns' friends

F loss is part of the unicorn's name

L ove is what the unicorns give us

O ctober is when they go for a walk

S assy unicorn

S caly unicorn.

Maisie Turner (7)

Drapers' Maylands Primary School, Harold Hill

Sloth Racer

Have you ever seen a racing sloth?
He coughs up a bit of broth,
The race begins, he's on his way,
And then he ends up on the bay,
Back through the rainforest,
He bumps into big Boris,
Boris invites him to the city,
He doesn't want to,
What a pity,
He goes back to the starting line,
And then he gets caught in a vine,
His name is Both,
The racing sloth,
What a pace,
What a race.

Amber Rose Robinson (9)
Drapers' Maylands Primary School, Harold Hill

Dancing Giraffe

D ancing
A round and around
N othing stops her
C ute she is
I n her sleep, she wants to dance
N icely she dances
G reat she is

G ia is my great giraffe
I really like her
R emarkably tall and very spotty
A nnoying sometimes she is
F airies she likes
F amous for tap-dancing
E ats all my food.

Amelia Ghinda (7)
Drapers' Maylands Primary School, Harold Hill

Magnificent Poem

M agnificent is always helpful

A nd never lazy or rude

G entle and adorable

N ever ferocious towards anybody

I n the night she glows in the dark

F antastic and clever

I love her so much

C ute and incredible

E verybody loves her

N ever scared of anything

T he best pet I have ever had.

Janice Jonah (7)
Drapers' Maylands Primary School, Harold Hill

Super Tiger

S o massive, it is as big as you
U p and down he soars
P ower is his weapon
E ating a lot every day
R attling tail always scares people

T errible claws and teeth
I nteresting wings with spikes
G reat muscles that break iron
E ager to eat with sharp teeth
R apidly wakes me up with hugs.

Finlay Gatdula (7)
Drapers' Maylands Primary School, Harold Hill

Super Hamster

S *woosh!*

U p and down

P erfect running

E ats too much food

R oar and roar

H eart beating

A s he always crashes

M eeting new friends

S uper happy

T rying his best

E ating sweets while having a rest

R esting, that's what he does.

Andrei Surdu (7)

Drapers' Maylands Primary School, Harold Hill

Unibun

U nlikely I know, but a unicorn bunny jumped out on me

N obody could know about this

I t was surprisingly cute and wanted a friend

B egging for a cuddle, I couldn't resist

U sually, I would be making my way to the ice cream shop

N ow my plans have changed, she is mine forever.

Molly McCluskey (7)
Drapers' Maylands Primary School, Harold Hill

Bumble Ear

B eautiful bees flying around
U p she goes
M aking honey for us
B eware of the bee's speed
L ooking at beautiful flowers
E verywhere she goes

E ating flowers and honey
A lways looking after bees
R emarkably fast.

Nicole Morozan (7)
Drapers' Maylands Primary School, Harold Hill

Pets, Pets, Peculiar Pets

Pets, pets, peculiar pets,
She's clever, but she's smelly.
She has long ginger locks,
Which I like to play with a lot.
She likes to eat cheese,
Whilst sitting on my knees,
But I hope she does not wee!
When she sleeps,
She loves to peep,
That's my cheeky kitty.

Maya Urrahman (9)
Drapers' Maylands Primary School, Harold Hill

My Flying Elephant

My messy elephant
Is a little bit elegant
By day he's an ordinary toy
But at night he's a flying elephant
He is so much better than my kite
Like a dream to me
And unlike Mr Bear, not so mean
My peculiar elephant
Oh, I do love you
I would never want to lose you.

Amelia Tumbridge (9)

Drapers' Maylands Primary School, Harold Hill

Crazy Lioncorn

Brian the lion is a skipping lioncorn
Other people think it's weird I have a lioncorn
I love my lazy, crazy lioncorn
She's sometimes grumpy, but also lovely
In the night, she takes a quick flight
One day, she dashed to the kitchen
And bashed into the wall.

Alveta Andriekute (7)
Drapers' Maylands Primary School, Harold Hill

Veronica The Vegan Crocodile

I'm a swamp swimmer,
In search of something to eat,
Not a flamingo, not a hippo,
But something on a leaf to feast,

I'm a carrot eater,
I'm a cucumber cruncher,
I'm a ferocious fighter,
I'm a deep diver.

What am I?

Raodat Adeshina (10)

Drapers' Maylands Primary School, Harold Hill

Big Eyes The Bush Baby

B ushes are too small for him, so he uses a tree instead

I like my bush baby

G igantic he is

E xtraordinary too

"Y ikes!" he says when a predator comes

E xcellent as well

S assy he is too.

Blake Tilbury (8)
Drapers' Maylands Primary School, Harold Hill

A Vegan Tiger

Have you ever seen a vegan tiger?
As he prowls around for prey,
Not meat,
Nor hay,
He hunts for salad all around,
In the bushes,
On the ground,
In the wind, trees twirl,
Slowly downwards,
Leaves whirl,
Salad's ready.

Kacie-Leigh Cooper (9)
Drapers' Maylands Primary School, Harold Hill

Panda Hero

P atient in person
A dorable for stroking
N ice to people
D ark at night
A nnoyed by bad guys

H elpful to people
E merald coloured
R ed volcano
O range trees.

Ayoola Agbaje (7)

Drapers' Maylands Primary School, Harold Hill

Super Cat

S uper cat
U p and up
P erfect to save you
E verywhere, everywhere you
R ide your carpet as you go

C an you fly so high?
A round the stars and sky
T onight.

Esther Oyemike (7)
Drapers' Maylands Primary School, Harold Hill

The Lightning Bunny

Have you ever seen a lightning bunny?
He blasts everything he sees,
He sneaks out at midnight,
And lives on a diet of cheese,
Some people are scared,
Some are not,
But does he care?
Not a lot.

Zain Urrahman (10)
Drapers' Maylands Primary School, Harold Hill

My Favourite Tiger

A limerick

I have a peculiar pet tiger,
That always lets me ride her,
I feed her raw meat,
Out in the street,
That's my peculiar tiger.

Rehan Ahmed (8)

Drapers' Maylands Primary School, Harold Hill

The Day I Met A Unikitty

The day I met a unikitty,
I saw him on my roof,
I thought he was cute until,
I realised he had hooves!

Sophie Colasanti (9)

Drapers' Maylands Primary School, Harold Hill

My Clever And Curious Cat!

I have a fluffy, adorable, tiny kitten,
He has a black and white body,
And also a pink nose and ears.
He is very clever because he always knows when
I'm giving him his food.
He is a clawed kitten, but he never does bite.
He looks very funny when I put him in his basket
because he hates going in his basket.
He always likes jumping around the house.
My lovely kitten is so incredibly curious about what
I do around the house.
He loves seeing me after school and he is scared of
my mum,
So when I come back, he jumps on me and thinks I
am a cuddly teddy bear.
I love my cute, fluffy, beautiful kitten.

Imaan Hussain (9)
Leigh Primary School, Washwood Heath

King Croc, King Croc

King Croc, King Croc,
You can bash through a lock.
King Croc, King Croc,
You're bigger than a clock.
King Croc, King Croc,
You're tougher than a rock.
King Croc, King Croc,
You have a big stomach.
King Croc, King Croc,
Should we have a feast?
King Croc, King Croc,
There is one in the east.
King Croc, King Croc,
Are you ready to eat?
King Croc, King Croc,
I fancy meat.
Yum, yum, yum in my tum.
King Croc, King Croc,
Are you ready to eat?

Raihan Ibrahim (10)
Leigh Primary School, Washwood Heath

My Pet Cat

I have a pet cat,
But she doesn't like bats,
She nips my book, sometimes she is kind,
I say, "Oh, Sally," but I still don't mind,
When I wash the dish,
She's hungry for fish,
When she plays, she flicks an elastic,
I say, "Sally, that was fantastic!"
That day when it was time for bed,
"Sally, I will see you." That's what I said.
I have a cat whose name is Sally,
Whenever I call her, it makes me happy.

Aleeza Khan (9)
Leigh Primary School, Washwood Heath

49

The Peculiar Paw

When I woke up this morning,
I started yawning,
Then I opened the door,
I saw a paw,
I stepped out for a closer look,
The paw gave me a book,
But when I looked back,
The paw was gone, there was only a sock,
I peeped inside,
Maybe the sock would give me a ride,
So I looked inside,
There was the paw,
The paw belonged to a yeti,
It was a good job it didn't start a war.

Malaika Rani Hussain (9)
Leigh Primary School, Washwood Heath

A Very Strange Pet

My pet is always running around like nuts,
She's cute but wild,
I always wonder what she's thinking,
All she eats is fish, fish, fish. Yuck!
She loves to sing, but never tries,
My pet has ginger fur and sapphire eyes,
My cute looking pet is very fun to play with,
I love my peculiar pet.
Do you like my peculiar pet?

Amaya Jabeen (10)
Leigh Primary School, Washwood Heath

Perfectly Peculiar Pet

My cat is only happy when we give her Dreamies,
When she dances our eardrums pop!
She loves her food like she loves me,
My parents say, "Stop!"
I say, "Yeah, me and my lovely cat,
Always stay together no matter what."

Ayesha Shabir (10)
Leigh Primary School, Washwood Heath

Scorbunny

What is this creature that lies beyond me,
It is a Pokémon you see.
Not a creature that you usually see,
Its skin as white a snow.
Its eyes as red as fire,
Its speed as fast as the wind.
It's a scorbunny.

Ayesha Ahmad (9)
Leigh Primary School, Washwood Heath

Kim The Parrot

This is Kim the parrot,
Who always munches on his carrot,
Kim always stares,
At the monkey who glares,
Kim is a boy,
And he loves playing with his log toy,
Are you sure this is Kim,
Or is it mean, old Tim?

Sanah Amir (9)
Leigh Primary School, Washwood Heath

Incredible Cat, Choices!

I n my house, I haven't seen my cat for a while

N ight is coming and I still can't see him

C reeping to my window and I look out for my cat in the horizon

R eally, is that my cat? I can't believe it!

E asily he fights off criminals and saves the day

D eep he flies beautifully and people chant his name, "Incredible Choices!"

I can't believe it! He can fly, he can walk with two feet, he can talk and he can fight!

B addies all running away and he flies up to my window

L ots of the baddies to get rid of forever, but he still saved the day!

E asily he flies to my window, he looks at me cutely and I stroke him and I say,

"**C** hoices, what a superhero!"

A nd so cool!

T o go we have to, but one thing... What a peculiar pet I have!

Majid Amponsem (10)

Limpsfield Junior School, Sheffield

My Lazy Ladybug

L azy ladybirds are one of a kind, sweet or not, I don't mind, all that matters, he's mine

A dorable and cute, what does it matter? He's my pet and that's all that matters

Z ebra is as black as my ladybird, but spots not stripes

Y es, I'm on his back, he falls asleep. *Boom! Crash!* We are down to the ground

L azy he is, but don't doubt him, he's very smart

A dorable she is, she's the best ever, okay

D angerous to be safe when you're on her back because *crash!*

Y ellow in autumn, he's more cute

B eautiful she is, but fast too

I ncredible at flying, she will win in a race

R ace, *boom!* She'll win

D oomed you are, you cheated, you're just jealous.

Amarn Zamil (8)
Limpsfield Junior School, Sheffield

Playful Panda

A nice sweet guy went on a walk one day,
To see a small panda lay and lay,
He stroked him kindly until one day,
He started playing all night, all day,
The guy was astonished by what he could do,
He could play a flute, that's what he could do!
The very next day, the man had a tumble,
The panda knew what to do,
So he grabbed his flute and ran until he was there,
He played his flute to a specific tune,
And everything turned out okay.
They had a hug or two and the day started to blur,
The man woke up to a big, loud noise,
And didn't know what to do,
He realised it was a dream, a good one indeed,
Months passed by as fast as you'd think,
As fast as a human's blink,
But he'll always remember the name of Playful
Panda, his superhero.

Sophie Rae Mitchell (10)
Limpsfield Junior School, Sheffield

Robbie The Ruing Robin

The lonely, lost robin sat upon a rusty, rickety log,
He was always a hog.
He only wanted a family and a home,
But he was only alone.
He saw birds cuddling in their house,
He loved to eat a mouse.
He flew over the town,
He burnt everything to the ground.
The people looked at fur dropping off his beautiful wings,
He became completely pink, one eye was winking.
As he saw predators coming for him,
A big version of him swooped down and saved him,
The rim of his hip was broken.
His heart started to mend when he saw his family,
They controlled his power and they lived happily.

Nirvana Phipps (10)
Limpsfield Junior School, Sheffield

Black Paw

My snake is very sinister,
He wants to kill Trump in front of his minister,
My snake is called a black panther snake,
It can poison you anytime,
Don't joke with him,
He doesn't like jokes,
If you get him mad, you will get blown up!
I live with Diamond and his mum, dad and sister,
They're all kind to me, but Diamond hates me,
I only play with Mustafe and Zack,
Diamond's friends are kind, but he is sinister,
Diamond killed Trump in front of his minister,
But Trump is fat, he poops out cats,
"LOL!" Diamond said,
I said, "Shut up!"

Diamond Haughton (9)
Limpsfield Junior School, Sheffield

Defeating The Enemy

As he watched the news,
He saw his arch-nemesis,
Yet again robbing a bank,
Hiss! He had to get him,
When will he learn? thought the cat.
Minutes after, it started to rain,
He looked at the cat,
Like it was his prey,
As strong as cement, fast as a flash,
In his Volkswagen,
Crash!
He quickly ran over,
The cat with the bags.
He didn't feel sorry, nor sad,
He knocked him out,
Yet again, Rote was arrested
But he knew,
What Rote would do,
But for now,
He would enjoy some catnip,
And rest until soon...

Feyzi Sozen (10)
Limpsfield Junior School, Sheffield

The Speaking Sparrow

R oaming, the sparrow found a friend
E vie was the name, she came to play
D etective, it was fun and they shared a bun

S parrows had fun, they hoped to play again
P irates were around the area however
A mazingly the sparrows saved the day
"R ight," Evie said, "do you wanna be friends?"
"R ight," the other sparrow said, "sure."
"O h yes," said Evie. "Do you wanna play
    detective?"
W ith the conclusion, they were best friends.

Kai Huxtable (10)

Limpsfield Junior School, Sheffield

Puffy Pandacorn

P roud, puffy and rainbow patterned
U sually rocking out with her guitar
F riendly, kind and caring
F luffy and cute like a kitten
Y ou would not believe your eyes

P uffy Pandacorn has aqua shoes
A lways ready to help the innocent
N ever gives up and
D efinitely always succeeds
A s cute as a baby unicorn
C upcake clothes, a magical horn and an aqua bow
O ccasionally she invites her friends
R eady to do some magic
N ever sad or lonely.

Briah Buch (8)
Limpsfield Junior School, Sheffield

My Scary Pet

Halloween Mystery is very mean,
When he eats beans he vomits at me.
Halloween Mystery is so ferocious,
That he hates flowers and roses.
Halloween Mystery likes mud,
He bathes in it like a pig while eating buns.
Halloween Mystery is very nice,
So for a treat, we go for ice cream.
Halloween Mystery is really great,
But I hate him because he won't eat cake.
Halloween Mystery is very dangerous,
He fights back when you touch his nose.
Halloween Mystery is wild, clawed and scaly,
When you touch him, you burn into his tummy.

Gabriel Quist (10)
Limpsfield Junior School, Sheffield

My DJ Turtle

H ennry is my favourite pet
E mma his girlfriend comes to pat him a lot
N ow he's growing up
N ow I think he's fattening up
R ight, he likes to listen to DJ Colin a lot
Y ou know he is terrible at dancing

P at him on his shell, he will like it a lot
O *uch!* He keeps chewing the wires a lot
T o me, I think he is everything you could dream of
T o me, he poos a lot
E at, eat a lot, he loses the plot
R ainbow shell is very typical.

Amelia Basharat
Limpsfield Junior School, Sheffield

Spidy Saves The Day

S uper Spidy makes his way to any crime

P rancing around tough on his break

I deas from you will make him save the day and you'll go phew!

D ressed up and Spidy is ready for his busy job

Y ou will always be saved by your microscopic friend Spidy

H e's on his way to save you and your family and friends

E asy job for Spidy, but not easy for humans

R unning fast through the town is useless for Spidy, he uses his skateboard

O ne last job for today, stop global warming.

Stanley Joe Priest (10)
Limpsfield Junior School, Sheffield

A Perfect Panda

Bounce, bounce! Here is the perfect panda,
I'm as cute as 5000 Boo dogs,
And as fluffy as a cloud.
Whoosh, whoosh!
There is a waterfall behind me.
I am a fairacorn,
I am as loud as bear, *grrr!*
I am as friendly as a fairy.
Bounce, bounce,
I have the world record for bouncing on a
trampoline.
Bye, that's it for today.
Crash! Oh no, my trampoline is broken,
I know, I can ask the fairy, they have magic,
Let's open the rainbow,
Abracadabra!

Savannah Johnson (9)
Limpsfield Junior School, Sheffield

World Domination And Demon Dolphin, Winter

D emon bottlenose dolphin
E ats delicious sardines
M arvellously cruel dolphin here
O n the water she would try domination
N ow she is on show she couldn't even try

D omination is what she wants
O h, how much she wants to be free
L ittle and cute is what you think
P rosthetic tail is what she has
H ere is a bad demon dolphin
I n the water she does flips
N ow she's here having fun, not taking over the world or being a demon!

Aimee Bridges (8)
Limpsfield Junior School, Sheffield

Avocado The Flying, Fast Turtle

I have a very strange turtle,
He can fly really fast and can also jump hurdles,
When he's sad, he lets out green tears,
He can't hear me very well because he has tiny ears,
Always kind and obedient,
We made a cake yesterday, but we accidentally left out an ingredient,
His room is very cluttered,
When I go tell him off, he quietly mutters,
He also has a secret,
He has a long, curly tail,
Today, Avocado's upset he can't go outside,
Because it's pouring rain and hail.

Ayaan Ali Ashraf (10)
Limpsfield Junior School, Sheffield

Parachuting Cute Red Panda

R ed pandas are iconic, but not this one!

"E ee!" That's what I heard one night and I looked outside

D ab! Dab! And I saw my red panda parachuting!

P anda, panda! I called him Parachuting Cute Red Panda

A fter that night, I got out of bed and jumped with him

"N aaa!" he screamed and his parachute deployed

D ad came out and said, "Huh? What? A parachuting pet!"

A fter 7.00am, Dad told Mum and that night we all did it!

Lucca Schofield (8)
Limpsfield Junior School, Sheffield

Creative Cat

Creative Cat is the superhero you should know,
She has a magical notebook and pen clipped to
her toe,
When she draws, her drawings come to life,
And once she saved her best friend from a knife,
Her tail extends so she can reach things as fast as
she can,
And she can poo chocolate for her owner Dan,
She loves to help out with her magical book,
So she draws helping robots to help her favourite
cook,
Her talent is walking on only two paws,
So she fought a robber using her legs as swords.

Rumaysa Saqib (10)
Limpsfield Junior School, Sheffield

The Sly, Sassy Snake!

S he goes for a sharp, sly kill every time

A s ghostly as her Slytherin past

S he patronisingly strangles you as you struggle to breathe

S assy Snake loves to flip and roll just like her lunatic self!

Y ashoomi, her name, nobody dares to speak it

S he slithers and slides across the slippery floor

N ow she begins her journey

A confusing twist

K *apow!* She's just bitten you

E *aow!* You're dead.

Henna Mortada (11)
Limpsfield Junior School, Sheffield

Idiot Horse

I rode to the apple at seven or eight,
And yelled to the manager running the place.

The manager said the shop was no more,
I replied, "Oh really, that's the case!"

It all started when I was up on the field,
Playing horse games with my mates.

I sprung up my wheel and drove downtown,
Thinking, *this won't do.*

So I drove as fast as I could,
Zoomed through the country in the time of a
launch,
That's what I could do.

William Fernando (10)
Limpsfield Junior School, Sheffield

Droxer The Boxer

Dragon-type Droxer will knock you out cold,
If he doesn't, he will shave your hair and make you really bald!
He breathes ice, water and snot!
If you stink, what will you do if you turn pink?
Droxer's scorpion tail is as deadly as a thorn,
But it is 12 times deadlier, so I wouldn't take his horn.
This boxer has Midas' golden touch,
He really would not like to live in a hutch.
He is way too dangerous for any human,
But I accidentally made the door open!

Haashir Saqib (9)

Limpsfield Junior School, Sheffield

Super Cat

S uper cat to the rescue
I ncredibly strong he is
R eally he can take down a villain in seconds

M arvellous, he is as strong as an elephant
E xtraordinary powers he's got
O n the way to save you
W ild he is when he gets mad
S uper cat to save the world

A wesome, strong creature he is

L umpy with muscle
O n the way to going home
T ough, he is punching beanbags.

Taylor Parnell (8)
Limpsfield Junior School, Sheffield

The Best Pet

M y pet is magical and amazing

I don't know how he has fire on him and it's a mystery

L ovely and kind, he gets you anything you want

O val and round he is

T eeth as sharp as a knife

H e is just tremendous

E xciting and fun he is

D og is tiny for his size, but fast for a little one

O ften he is hyper and wants me to play ball

G rowl, he does growl until he gets his food.

Ethan Baxter (8)

Limpsfield Junior School, Sheffield

Rocket Ship Raccoon!

R ocket Ship Raccoon
O ver the moon
C atching the star
K angaroo jumping on the moon
E choing loud
T all when I jump

S o, so high
H op, hop, hop!
I like to jump
P ounce, pounce!

R olling on the floor
A bright sun moving
C hasing the star
C hasing
O h, oh, oh!
O ver the Earth
N ever been this high.

Ogechi Ejiogu (9)

Limpsfield Junior School, Sheffield

Peculiar Evie

Well let me tell you about Evie O'Sullivan
She is a dog that likes socks for breakfast
She chews and chews until they are all gone
Sometimes she may have more than one
She runs and runs until she gets tired
Running around until she decides to stop
Then she might come and lick my lollipop
She snores so much after a run
After a sleep she will have a lot of fun
That's my dog, she is Evie
I love her and she loves me.

Darciee Malcolm O'Sullivan (11)
Limpsfield Junior School, Sheffield

Super Dancing Joey

T appy was a super dancing joey
A superhero, in fact, he kills villains
P eople from all over the world called him for rescue
P eople called him Super Joey to the rescue
Y es, he's here! How did you get here?

D oesn't like cars
A jopatation I like
N onsense, there's no such thing
C ourageous Cat, my psychic
E nemies here I come!

Abigail Grace Nicholls (10)
Limpsfield Junior School, Sheffield

The Superhero Cat

S unday morning there was a superhero cat
U nique, special cat
P layful, beautiful pet
E very day the superhero cat went everywhere
R abbits are his favourite friends, sometimes he
  eats them
H e is always happy
E aster is his favourite time, he loves it
R aspberries are his favourite food, even though
  he's a cat
O lives, he hates olives, he gulps them out.

Soraya Abdou (8)
Limpsfield Junior School, Sheffield

Turbo Tortoise

There is a turbo tortoise,
With colourful stripes like butterflies' wings.
I can talk like a human,
But only my owner knows!
Shhh! People think that I'm so slow,
But I'm really, really speedy.
I am the cleverest tortoise in the world,
Ask me any question and I'll answer it.
The tremendous turbo tortoise,
Has a brain like an intelligent robot,
My pet is the best pet ever.

Beth Aston (8)
Limpsfield Junior School, Sheffield

My Messy Cat, Mandy!

M y cat is unique!

A s she flies to the moon, she howls and she runs as fast as the wind!

N ow you may not know what I'm talking about, so let me tell you!

D id you know she has devil horns, vibrant wings, a dark blue and light blue fur and usually has mud all over her?

Y ou should probably get one. I usually find them in the forest and they are very colourful!

Amina Mamboleo (9)

Limpsfield Junior School, Sheffield

The Weird Snake!

My snake is very weird you see,
He has legs, it's very scary!
He can also dig, just stay away from him!
He has a blue pattern under his skin!
He is also longer than a car,
He's that dangerous that it's safer on a star!
He's normally looking for prey,
So if he sees you, run away!
The cool thing about him is that he can fly,
I didn't want him, why?

Roman Mitchell (7)
Limpsfield Junior School, Sheffield

Derik The Snake

Derik sat down thinking of past events,
As he sat there, he thought of sneaking into a vent,
He got up and hissed to the bank,
But there wasn't a bank,
He was put in cuffs and he found some fluff,
As he was let out, he rolled about,
But then he found a sprout,
He ate the sprout,
He was poisoned, but luckily he survived,
But he almost died...

Alfie Gibson (10)
Limpsfield Junior School, Sheffield

My Adorable Pet!

D olphin is so cute
O ver and down, splashing everyone
L ove her, she is so unique!
P lay with her, she'll love it, you'll see!
H igh up in the sky, she is so adorable
I take her home every day, she is my best friend!
N ice and snuggly, faithful and exuberant, I'm happy she's mine!

Emily Nicholls (7)
Limpsfield Junior School, Sheffield

My Colourful Pet Dog

L azy dog has colourful eyes

A mazing dog, but it barks loud

Z oo, it likes living in a zoo, it's that loud

Y *elp!* she cries

L ittle dog is kind

O n the field is a wild dog

S o she is fluffy

E xciting and amazing she is

R ainbow eyes, sparkly and bright.

Aishah Rashid (7)

Limpsfield Junior School, Sheffield

The Rainbow Pup

R ainbow is the colour that my animal likes
A mazing when you feed him and he can fly
I nside, outside, working everywhere
N aughty always when he can't fly
B oring he is when he can't fly
O ld and young, he is really cool and colourful
W ow, he is a good pet, it's good I have him.

Ollie Staniforth
Limpsfield Junior School, Sheffield

The Flying Dog

Fly! Fly! Fly! Here comes Fly Dog!
She goes up and up in the sky!
She's cute, she's nice and kind,
She lives in a dog treehouse on her own,
She goes on her own everywhere,
She went down, down and down!
She went to the dog shop,
And she went on a walk on her own,
Then she went back home and had a rest.

Charis Weston (8)
Limpsfield Junior School, Sheffield

The Smartest Lion In The World

There was a lion called Jeff,
He liked going to the park,
And he was also smart.
He could also fly to the sky,
And also became Prime Minister,
And could have been sinister.
Some people just think he was ordinary,
But he was not,
And sometimes lost the plot.
And he was as large as a giant pyramid.

Bilal Abrouche (9)
Limpsfield Junior School, Sheffield

My Kind Kangadog

My Kangadog,
Is as skinny as a log.
My Kangadog,
Has big round ears,
It's very easy for him to hear.
My Kangadog,
Wakes up in the dark,
And does an emotional bark.
My Kangadog,
Has a very cute cry,
Big grey clouds,
Pop up from his mind.
My Kangadog,
Says goodbye.

Elisia Nkereko (9)
Limpsfield Junior School, Sheffield

Rummy The Dog

Every day Rummy the dog is lazy,
And she is pretty crazy.
She is made of candy,
Also, her friend is Mandy.
She is candy, so that is the reason everyone says,
She is incredible and edible.
Shooting stars coming directly out of her ears,
She is funny and her tummy is plump,
Also very furry.

Minsa Farhan (8)
Limpsfield Junior School, Sheffield

My Little Rabbit That Can Play...

F antastic little rabbit I have

O nly I have one

O n the day I got it, I found out

T hat it can play football!

B ecause it is so amazing

A ll I want to do is learn from her

L ots of energy she has

L oving, caring and very sporty.

Lilly Smith (7)

Limpsfield Junior School, Sheffield

My Zeleopard Dog

My zeleopard dog,
Is shaped like a log,
Although she is agile,
Sometimes she is very fragile,
My zeleopard dog,
Is as lazy as a sloth,
Because she doesn't like to catch a moth,
My zeleopard dog is a very special pet,
It's a shame you haven't met her yet.

Ruby Lockwood (9)
Limpsfield Junior School, Sheffield

Super Rainbow Rabbit

On to the rescue!
Here he comes, Super Rabbit!
Smashing and crashing into tall buildings,
Not looking where he is going,
Finally gets to the mission,
Helps the person who is hurt,
Completes the mission and gets back home,
"What a dangerous mission," he said.

Zak Zahid (8)
Limpsfield Junior School, Sheffield

DJ Panda

Abracadabra, here is the DJ Panda,
DJ Panda is fluffy like a cloud,
And he can live up to 83 years, wow!
Bang! Sorry, that was my crazy jetpack,
In the night, sneaking out,
But my mum and dad don't know I'm a DJ,
That's why I'm called DJ Panda.

Hannah Chitopo (8)
Limpsfield Junior School, Sheffield

All About My Peculiar Pet

Have you met my pet? She is amazing,
She has lots of amazing things about her,
She has a unicorn horn, purple mask,
Blue cape and headphones,
And she loves rainbows and trampolines and carrots,
And has a rainbow above her head all the time.
Her name is Fluffy Rabbit.

Lillie Greaves (8)
Limpsfield Junior School, Sheffield

Kitty Catur

Kitty goes on Twitty to see what was in pity,
She sees a dog going to the bog eating a log,
Catur breaks the law by licking her paw and
breaks someone's jaw,
She sees a pen and made a den,
In the house was a mouse eating cheese,
Kitty was pleased, she had a feast.

Alayah Khan (10)
Limpsfield Junior School, Sheffield

Cuddles

My furry pet is adorable, you'll see,
The way it sparkles, you will be in a rabbit mystery!
My pet is a cute and clever rabbit called Cuddles,
She's a colourful rainbow and gentle,
But don't get her shampoo muddled!
She has beautiful wings and huge lumps.

Scarlett Crowther (8)
Limpsfield Junior School, Sheffield

Tarantula Pig! The Many-Legged Guinea Pig

Tarantula Pig... the guinea pig that has eight legs,
Very strange, but very grumpy,
Sometimes very inquisitive,
He can be grumpy too.

Tarantula Pig was a guinea pig,
But he got eaten by a tarantula,
So now he has many legs,
And is... Tarantula Pig!

Jacob Dunning (10)
Limpsfield Junior School, Sheffield

My Incredible Pet

Hoko likes to fly,
But this time he does not want to try.
Hoko is brave,
But Hoko says if he tries, he will go to his grave.
Hoko has a teacher who said, "Let's do a short flying session,
Who knows, it might give you some passion."

Ahmed Syed (9)
Limpsfield Junior School, Sheffield

Banana Gorilla

If you want a banana, the gorilla will not let you,
Also, he eats bananas, so you can't have one.
Well, if you are lucky, you will get to see him put his bananas down,
He is also very clumsy,
Do not touch his skin or you will turn into a banana.

Jacob Duffy (8)
Limpsfield Junior School, Sheffield

Clever Cat

My pet is a super cat,
It wears a cape and an eye mask.
My pet is brown,
It is as fluffy as a cloud.
At night, she whizzes off,
And goes to fight bad guys.
One night, I jumped on her back,
And she whizzed off through the night.

Shafiyah Amina Bashir (8)
Limpsfield Junior School, Sheffield

Let's Go!

Cheetahs run fast and birds fly high,
Do you ever wonder about mixing them together?
To make a birdcher, a birdcher!
Birdcher! Birdcher! How about dirbcher?
Have you ever mixed two animals?
Like birdcher or even dirbcher?

Israa Miah (10)

Limpsfield Junior School, Sheffield

Ellie And The Fun Day

I have a pet called Ellie,
She is a superhero,
She loves going to the park,
Let's go have some fun.
Off to the park we go,
Oh no, Ellie,
There is a cat stuck,
Yay, you got him,
Let's go home.

Faye Bennett (10)
Limpsfield Junior School, Sheffield

Pumpkin

P umpkin is a singing guinea pig
U nbelievable talent
M arvellous music
P umpkins are his favourite food
K ittens try to eat him
I nteresting
N ow he is amazing!

Florence Joel-Drennan (9)
Limpsfield Junior School, Sheffield

Sploge

S he loves me like honey
P *uff, puff,* she puts make-up on
L ove is all she gives me
O range is just like Sploge
G reat she is
E legant she is with her make-up.

Riley Marsland (8)

Limpsfield Junior School, Sheffield

Aubameyang Dog

Bang! Goal! One, two, three,
Aubameyang comes to play,
Stay, just pass and call,
Don't give up, don't touch,
He would certainly not live in a hut,
He's very good, but not dumb.

Aahil Khan (8)
Limpsfield Junior School, Sheffield

Super Dolco

Super Dolco sees his fans,
Goes around to meet his fans,
Shows his fans his powers,
People go crazy seeing his powers,
He goes to the park to hide,
Too big to hide, so he has to ride.

Muskaan Hussain (11)
Limpsfield Junior School, Sheffield

Cowboy Panda

Abracadabra, here's the cowboy panda,
He's so fantastic,
He can live up to 83 years,
Cowboy Panda is fluffy like a cloud,
And he is a magician,
He can run super fast.

Joshua Smith (8)
Limpsfield Junior School, Sheffield

Beller The Basketball Player

B eautiful and unique
E aster bunny
L ovely bunny
L azy sometimes when she is tired
E aster is her birthday
R aspberries are her favourite!

Heidi Rodgers (8)
Limpsfield Junior School, Sheffield

The Cobra With The Cat

The cobra with a cat has no doubts,
The cobra is rapidly fast,
But the cat is nothing without a doubt.
The cobra is as skinny as a pencil,
But the cat is as puffy as a pillow.

Esmond Thompson (9)
Limpsfield Junior School, Sheffield

Devil Dog

Ah! Ah! Ah! Here comes Devil Dog,
He has a feisty instinct,
He is destructive, bad, unbeatable!
The only thing that can beat him is pure good!
He can swim in lava.

Akira Wilkinson (8)
Limpsfield Junior School, Sheffield

Jimmy The Draglon

My name is Jimmy,
You might think I'm scary, but I'm not.
I give people nightmares because I look evil when
I'm not.
P.S. I'm a dragon/lion called a Draglon.

Zak Fox (10)
Limpsfield Junior School, Sheffield

Weird Dog

Works for a weird business,
He writes messy,
Makes sure you laugh,
Bad at his job,
Very lazy and doesn't get paid,
Isn't able to walk,
Has no food.

Madison Brough (8)
Limpsfield Junior School, Sheffield

Duckasaurus

B read is a very special pet
R eally loud
E ats lots of bread, yummy!
A mazingly giant and kind
D uck hats are his favourite.

Darcie Wake (9)
Limpsfield Junior School, Sheffield

Funny Cat

Has funny, yellow duck feet,
Funny, spotty neck,
Brown, soft fur,
So always try to find her,
So look out, she is really funny!

Ikhlas Mah (8)
Limpsfield Junior School, Sheffield

A Bird? A Plane? Flying Fifi!

Flying Fifi is a little pup,
She's a furball full of fluff,
When she flies up high,
She goes, "Ruff! Ruff! Ruff!"
People see her from down there,
Flying high, soaring through the air,
Flying high, in forests seeing bears,
I make her jump by giving a scare.
But now where is Fifi?
Oh, where, oh, where?
Her fur is as smooth as silk,
She sees cats drinking milk!
She wears pink goggles,
They make a sound that goes *boggle, boggle!*
Her scarf is really soft,
Once it got muddy while she was at a bog,
She plays with her marvellous friend, Magnificent
Mog.
People call her a pup,
With really good luck,

Oh yes, it's Flying Fifi.
When me and Fifi are walking,
And we see a squirrel,
Fifi feels apprehensive,
And her ears start flapping.

Tabasem Azizi (8)

Oakington Manor Primary School, Wembley

The Strongest Dragon Ever

D arkness it is, soaring in the skies
A ctive, it would play all day if it could
R ough, every day he gets himself dirty like he normally would
K inaesthetic, that's the only way to teach him!

M arvellous, but never perfect
I ndigo, that would be the perfect pet for me
D angerous, it breathes midnight blue fire
N ever ever would it get hurt as he is one of a kind!
I ntelligent, smart, courageous, what good features
G o, go, go! As fast as lightning!
H e never gives up and never lets me down
T o rate my pet, it's 99.7 percent.

Promise Soda (8)
Oakington Manor Primary School, Wembley

Lazy Lion

I went to Kenya for a safari
Then I saw the lazy lion
There it was, munching on grass
Every swallow equals a fart
This was an amazing scene
Oh look, it did a wee
The whooshy wind made his mane flap
This really was a lazy cat
There it was with its pot belly
I wanted to touch it as it looked like jelly
The grass was trembling with fear
As the lion's mouth came near
There was the lion with all its might
This lion was too fat to fight
It should do a poo
Oh it did! Whoop de doo!

Maximilian Paulo Lule (9)
Oakington Manor Primary School, Wembley

Percy The Panda

Percy the panda eats bamboo,
She hates the smell of smelly glue,
She loves the forest,
Where her friend, Bear, eats porridge,
You'll find her in China climbing trees,
She doesn't like broccoli,
She is black and white,
If you try to hit her there is a problem,
I'm telling you, she knows how to fight,
She stays up at night just to find food,
She knows she has to be good,
But decides not to do good,
"Do good," she always says to friends,
She pays her friends with food.

Fathima Begum (8)
Oakington Manor Primary School, Wembley

The Lazy Stan

L ikes food and does anything to get it

A rtist at eating mammoth, monstrous food sizes

Z ack the magician can't beat the lazy lad, Stan

Y ummy food he likes, if you don't give him some, he fights

S almon is Stan's nice meal, if you give him some, he will make a colossal deal

T itan for his height and his wonderful sight

A n excellent eater, he won't like it if you put on the heater

N ot the rudest, but mostly not the slowest.

Azaan Asim (8)
Oakington Manor Primary School, Wembley

Marvellous Angel

M assive, cute pet
A gile and sassy cat
R adical, tame tiger
V enomous, fluffy snake
E xtraordinary, lazy sloth
L iberating, calm koala
L onely, gentle Labrador
O rdinary, wild kangaroo
U nderwater orca
S caly, poisonous cobra

A dorable, tiny dog
N atural, breathtaking flamingo
G olden-orange orangutan
E merging, dangerous lion
L oving, hugging squirrels.

Quiana Quaye-Murray (8)
Oakington Manor Primary School, Wembley

Super Cat And Bomb Dog Save The Day

Slowly and calmly some people were walking,
Came past an enormous crane from where
builders were talking,
Billy the builder was thinking where to move the
crane,
Down came a noise where the people were
chatting,
Suddenly, the gigantic crane came crashing down,
Super Cat and Bomb Dog flew as fast as lightning
to save the day,
Difficult it was, but the superheroes made it on
time,
Bomb Dog released to fire himself, he dived quickly
and grabbed the people to save the day.

Ubaidullah Butt (9)

Oakington Manor Primary School, Wembley

Dangerous Billy

D angerous creature is here and it's special to me
A sloth is my pet with monkey ears and a cool hat
N o one likes it
G orgeous at night, it's ready to play with me
E xtraordinary creature is ready
R oars when it's angry
O h, cute pet, its name is Billy
U sually insecure when it's alone, but it can fight
S limy Billy is always slimy and anyone who annoys him, get ready to be slimy.

Musa Nadim (9)
Oakington Manor Primary School, Wembley

Fluffy The Rabbit

F un as always like a butterfly
L aughable and exciting as well as funny
U nique and adorable
F urry and soft like a pillow
F idgety like you got ants in your pants
Y ou will always love Fluffy the rabbit

R uns away like a flash
A gile like a cheetah in the wind
B eautiful like nature
B usy like a bee
I ncredible in every way
T roublesome every day.

Courtney Rebecca Jackson (9)
Oakington Manor Primary School, Wembley

The Rocking Rock Star

R eally rocking all day long
O nly people who rock this place
C razy concert going on around here
'K ay, only peculiar pets allowed who rock

S orry, 18 or older you need to be to come
T he concert has just started, come check it out
A round him are people surrounding him
R eally you need to check him out now
S tars shooting everywhere he goes.

Jameelah Abyan (8)
Oakington Manor Primary School, Wembley

The Best Dog

T he dog can hit hard like Iron Man
H ench dog as always
E ats so much like a big boy

B ig and lovely, but scary
E gg he loves the most
S trong as a boxer
T oo good at jumping like a cat

D igs every day because he likes ants
O ut all day long like a human
G ood and listens every day.

Yasin Mumtaz Ahmed (8)
Oakington Manor Primary School, Wembley

The Ferocious Alligator!

A gile and wild
L urking down the river
L azy enough
I t could eat you up in one gulp!
G iant scales
A ctually not the type of pet you would have
T all and gloopy
O n the riverbank sunbathing
R un before he sees you!

Who is the mysterious creature?

Answer: Alligator.

Ojashwee Maharjan (9)
Oakington Manor Primary School, Wembley

The Butterfly Called Princess!

P rincess parties all night

R ight till the sunlight is out

I nsects dance to her beat

N o one can have her because she is unique

C an she do tricks, like throw sticks?

E veryone treats her like royalty

S he loves to draw just like me

S he is a furry baby and she is as funny as a monkey.

Saleeha Mirza (8)

Oakington Manor Primary School, Wembley

Tommy The Clever Horse

T ame and helpful horse
O val tail helps him balance
M arvellous, brown horse
M agnificent, furry horse
Y oung, clever horse.

Arham Ahmed Awan (8)
Oakington Manor Primary School, Wembley

My Dog, Murphy

M urphy is my pet dog
Y ou would love him so much

P erfect in many ways
E xcellent friend except he's lazy sometimes
T oo cute and beautiful

D elicious treats are his favourite
O utside he doesn't like rain or thunder
G enuinely, the best dog ever.

Lennon Snitch (10)
The Harbour School, Wilburton

Frogy Bogy

F erocious and funny
R aging, ridiculous
O utstanding obstacle
G ory
Y ummy, yuck

B rilliant bog
O range eye October
G round grabber
Y ou should yell.

Jesse Nunley Towers (11)
The Harbour School, Wilburton

Marmite!

M arvellous cat
A nnoying my parents
R unning around and
M iaowing all the time
I gnorant
T ired all the time
E nergetic too.

Caleb Harrington (9)
The Harbour School, Wilburton

Bentley

B est cat
E ver!
N ever sits still
T ame and soft
L oves his food
E ating all the time
Y es, he's the best!

Lewis Schreiber (7)
The Harbour School, Wilburton

My Cat, Bobby

B eautiful cat
O ff out for the day too
B uy an Xbox
B usy, busy
Y ay! A new Xbox to play on.

Jack Garner-Stovin (8)
The Harbour School, Wilburton

Beegu! The Alien Pet That Crashed Here!

B eautiful
E xcellent alien
E ver bright
G lowing
U nder the stars.

Joey Mattless (8)
The Harbour School, Wilburton